Oh, Kitty!

Oh, Kitty!

Bel Mooney

Illustrated by
Margaret Chamberlain

containing *I Don't Want To!*
I Can't Find It! and *It's Not Fair!*

DEAN

I Don't Want To! first published 1985
I Can't Find It! first published 1988
It's Not Fair! first published 1989
This edition first published in 1992 by Dean,
A division of Reed International Books Ltd
Michelin House, 81 Fulham Road, London SW3 6RB
Text copyright © Bel Mooney 1985, 1988 and 1989
Illustrations copyright © Margaret Chamberlain
1985, 1988 and 1989

A CIP catalogue record for this book is
available from the British Library

ISBN 0 603 55078 9

Printed in Great Britain by The Bath Press

I don't want to!

For Alice, Maisie
Kitty, Heather and Grace

Contents

I don't want to
Clean my Teeth

Once there was a little girl called Kitty who didn't want to clean her teeth. Each night she would cry and scream and throw her toothbrush to the ground. One night she even wrote her name in toothpaste on the bathroom wall. "I *won't* clean my teeth," she said.

Kitty's mum was cross. "If you don't

clean your teeth they will all fall out,"
she said.

"I don't care," said Kitty. "I want to
have a mouth with no teeth in it, just
like Grandad's."

"How will you be able to chew your
food?" asked Mum.

"I will only eat soup and Instant
Whip and porridge," said Kitty, "because they don't need any chewing!"

That night Kitty went to bed without
cleaning her teeth. She put her finger in
her mouth and tried to get out a piece of
meat that was stuck in her tooth. It
always made Mum angry when she did
that. Kitty could still taste the sugar on
the apple pie she had for pudding, and
the delicious chocolatey taste of the
cocoa.

"Yum, yum," she said. "I like to
taste my tea. When you clean your teeth
all the time you can only taste boring old
toothpaste. I don't believe all the things
the grown-ups tell you about sweets

making your teeth fall out – and anyway, I don't CARE!"

And Kitty took a sweet from the packet she had hidden under her pillow, and chewed it happily. Then she turned over and fell asleep.

Kitty started to dream. She dreamt that she was walking in a huge, dark wood, where the trees grew thickly and no birds sang. Suddenly she heard a loud cry. She ran towards the sound, and there in a clearing she saw Little Red Riding Hood with the wolf. But it wasn't Little Red Riding Hood who was crying, it was the wolf!

Red Riding Hood kicked the wolf sharply on his knee and laughed. "I'm not afraid of you any more, because you're just a silly old toothless has-been," she shouted.

The wolf turned to Kitty and she saw

that it was true. He had no teeth.

"Where are your teeth?" Kitty asked.

"They all fell out," the wolf sighed. "I didn't ever clean them after I had eaten the children and animals, when I was the Big Bad Wolf. Now I can't be a Big Bad Wolf because who ever heard of a Big Bad Wolf without any teeth?" The wolf started to cry. "The other day," he sobbed, "I tried to frighten the Three Little Pigs, but they just laughed and said that when I blew their house down they'd give me some rice pudding for my gums."

Red Riding Hood poked him in the eye with her finger. "Yah, stupid old gummy!"

"Anybody whose job is being horrid has to have teeth," said the wolf sadly. "Otherwise people aren't afraid of him."

Kitty gasped. "But I want to be horrid," she said.

"Then you mustn't let your teeth fall out," said the wolf.

Red Riding Hood led him away, sticking twigs into his back, and laughing all the time.

Kitty woke up from the dream, and rushed into the bathroom. She was cleaning her teeth very carefully when Mum came in.

"There's my good little girl," smiled Mum, patting Kitty gently upon her head. "Now you'll have pretty white teeth when you're a big girl, won't you, darling?"

But Kitty looked into the bathroom mirror, and snarled. It wasn't a pretty girl *she* saw in there. It was the nastiest, fiercest wolf in the world.

I don't want to
Eat my Vegetables

Daniel and Kitty were brother and sister, but they didn't like each other very much. Kitty thought Daniel was Mum's favourite, because he did all the right things and never got into trouble. Dan thought Kitty was silly and a nuisance – and he was always telling her so. But only when Mum wasn't listening.

The worst times were mealtimes. This was because Dan always ate everything on his plate, but Kitty pushed hers away and asked for ham or biscuits. She wouldn't eat anything else.

"Oh good, it's cabbage – my favourite," said Dan one day.

"Yuk, cabbage," said Kitty, who

16

especially never wanted to eat her vegetables. She always called them *veggy-troubles* because they got her into trouble.

"If you don't eat up all your vegetables there'll be no pudding for you," warned Mum.

"Horrible, horrible!" shouted Kitty, and banged her fork on her plate.

Dad groaned. "Not all this again," he said. "Why are mealtimes always so awful in this house?"

"Because Kitty won't eat her vegetables, of course," said Daniel, putting the last piece of cabbage into his mouth.

"I don't want to eat my yukky veggy-troubles," shouted Kitty.

Instead of getting cross, Mum tried to persuade her. "Cabbage, carrots, green beans and cauliflower are good for you. They make you big and strong," she said.

"*You'll* never be bi-ig; *you'll* always be litt-le," sang Dan.

Kitty started to cry. She jumped down from the table and ran outside.

She looked around the garden, and thought. Grass. Nasturtium leaves. All green. She took her toy wheelbarrow, and filled it with handfuls of grass and nasturtium leaves, and stirred it all round with a stick. Then she proudly pushed the wheelbarrow back into the kitchen. "Look," she said, "I've grown

some veggy-troubles of my own. Shall I eat them?"

"Of course not, darling," said Mum.

But Dad stood up, looked closely at the green stuff to make sure it was safe, and said, "I don't see why not. Shall I cook it for you, Kitty-Kat?"

He poured boiling water from the kettle into a pan, then tipped in handfuls of the leaves and grass. He stirred it all round with a wooden spoon, and asked Kitty if she wanted some salt.

Dan started to giggle as Dad took the

colander, drained Kitty's vegetables,
and asked her to pass her plate.

"Now sit in your chair," Dad said,
putting the plate in front of Kitty – who
thought that the green mixture looked
awful. "There you are. You don't like
our vegetables, but I'm sure you'll like
your own."

Kitty took her spoon, and looked at
her plate. Then she saw Mum and Dan
laughing.

"I'll show them," she thought, "I

will."

Very slowly, she lifted her spoon to
her mouth and chewed. Mum and Dan
stopped laughing, but still smiled.

Kitty ate some more, and they
stopped smiling. Mouthful after
mouthful disappeared, until the plate

21

was completely empty. At last Kitty put down her spoon.

"That was dee-licious," she said. Mum, Dad and Daniel just stared. "I feel stronger and bigger already. But perhaps next time I'll eat your boring old veggy-troubles instead, because mine take *so* long to collect."

And from then on – she always did.

I don't want to
Wash

"Daniel was such a good boy when he was your age," Mum said. "He used to go upstairs after tea to wash his face, and *without being told!*"

Kitty didn't believe it. But Dan sat at the table with a smile that said, "Oh what a good boy am I."

Kitty gave her big brother a dirty look. It was a very dirty look indeed because her face was all smeared with jam and soil. This was because she had run into the garden in the middle of tea and put her nose in the earth to see if she could smell the worms. She already had jam on her face and hands. So the earth stuck to the jam, and Kitty rubbed her hands on her face to see if she could get it off, before Mum saw her.

23

Now Kitty was a terrible sight, but still she said, "I don't want to wash my face."

"Do you like looking like a grub?" asked Mum.

"Yes, I do," said Kitty. "I want to be dirty. I like being dirty. I won't wash ever again!"

"Ugh, horrible!" said Dan. "When you walk down the road everyone will run away."

"Why?" asked Kitty.

"Because of the awful *smell*," laughed

Dan, and ran away when Kitty chased him round the table.

Mum put her head in her hands. At last she looked up and sighed. "All right! You *stay* dirty!" She took Daniel upstairs to have his bath.

After a few minutes Kitty was bored in the kitchen. She crept upstairs, and listened outside the bathroom door. Daniel was making happy splashing noises, and Mum was talking to him quietly, and suddenly Kitty felt very sticky and uncomfortable. There were crumbs in her hair, and dirt on her arms, and earth on her tee-shirt, and her legs itched where she had rolled in the grass. Kitty felt dirty. She was jealous of Dan for getting clean.

She hid round the corner when Mum took Daniel across the landing into his room – all wrapped cosily in the big white towel. Then Kitty slipped into the bathroom. The bath was still full of water, and Dan's best boat was floating in it, as well as two ducks. The boats and ducks looked clean. The bathwater was warm and inviting.

Kitty took off her shoes and socks, then stopped. Only her face, legs and arms were dirty, that was all. The rest of her was covered by the shorts and tee-shirt, but *they* were covered with jam and earth.

Kitty had an idea. She would wash her clothes. So she jumped into the bath

still wearing them, and lay down with the boat and ducks. Some of the water splashed over the side, but Kitty hoped it would clean the floor.

She grabbed the soap, but it didn't make enough foam. So she poured the whole of the bottle of shampoo down her front, and rubbed it into her clothes. That was better.

The flannel was on the washbasin, and Kitty couldn't reach it. So she pulled down the small white towel, dipped it in the bathwater, and used it to rub at her face, arms and legs. That was better, and anyway, it wasn't like a *real* wash.

Then Kitty looked at the dirty shoes and socks lying on the floor, and thought they needed a clean too. She climbed out of the bath, holding the wall so she would not slip, and threw the shoes and socks into the bath. The shoes floated. They were much better than Dan's silly old boat.

Just as Kitty was scrubbing at the muddy shoes with the smallest cleaning thing she could find – Dan's toothbrush – Mum came into the bathroom to pull out the plug. She seemed very surprised. All she could say was, "Oh Kitty. Oh KITTY!"

Kitty pointed to her clean pink face. "I did have my wash, Mum," she said.

I don't want to
Go to Bed

Kitty loved bedtime stories, and drinking chocolate, and cuddling down with her favourite teddy bear, but she hated the idea of bedtime. She didn't like to think that the day was over, and there was no more time for fun and games, and she would be left all alone in the dark.

Kitty didn't like the dark. She never told Mum and Dad, because she was proud of being *tough* – not like her soppy cousin Melissa, who was nervous of animals, insects, quiet places, and *everything*. No, Kitty would not tell anyone she ever felt afraid. Still, she was just a teeny bit nervous of the shadows in her room when the light was out, even though Mum always switched on

29

the little lamp on the landing outside.

Some evenings she cried and said, "It's too early." Other times she whined, "But Daniel's still up. It's not fair!", so that Mum had to explain – for the hundredth time – that Daniel was older, and so went to bed a bit later. And there were some nights when she went to hide. But no matter what new brilliant hiding places she found, Mum always spotted her, and tickled her, and carried her upstairs to her room.

One night Kitty was particularly

cross because Mum and Dad were going out to the cinema, and had asked a new babysitter to come. "You must be very helpful to poor Christine," Mum said, "because she hasn't been before and she is only seventeen."

Mum told Daniel to play quietly in his room, and said she would put Kitty in her pyjamas half an hour earlier than usual.

Kitty was cross, but there was no chance to run away. She was into her pyjamas and in bed before she could say, "Don't want to . . .", and when the doorbell rang Mum kissed her and went downstairs.

Kitty heard her talking quietly to the babysitter in the hall, and just managed to catch the words, ". . . safely in bed." She frowned. "But I don't want to go to bed," she muttered to herself. "And I jolly well won't. I'll hide – right now!"

She jumped out of bed, ran into the spare room (being careful to leave the door open behind her) and crouched down behind the bed. "When the silly old babysitter goes into my room to check me and say good night, she'll get a surprise," Kitty thought. "Serve them right for putting me to bed so early." And she settled down to wait for the fuss.

Christine the babysitter came upstairs, tiptoed past Kitty's room, and went in to make sure Daniel was putting himself to bed. She was glad that Kitty's

room was so quiet. She did not look in. She went downstairs again, and turned on the television.

Kitty waited to be found. She waited and waited. Then she yawned. At last, tired of waiting, she curled up on the floor and fell asleep.

When Mum and Dad came back from the cinema, Christine told them that Kitty had not woken up, and so they too tiptoed past her bedroom door. They went to bed. The house was silent.

Outside an owl hooted, and Kitty woke up. For a moment, she did not know where she was. The floor was hard. For a moment she thought she was dreaming about a dark, dark prison, with dark, dark shadows, and a strange four-legged monster called the Sparebed, which towered over her. Then Kitty heard the owl again and knew she wasn't dreaming. "MMUUUUUUUM!" she cried.

Mum ran into the room. "Oh Kitty,

what are you doing in *here?*" she asked, picking Kitty up and carrying her into her own room.

Kitty's bed was soft, white and warm. Her teddy bears sat in a row with their backs to the wall, and her toy dog waited inside the bed. All the things Kitty loved best were in her room: the wooden train set, the butterfly mobile above the bed, the painted mirror, and her new castle, filled with little plastic people.

"Isn't your own bed best of all?"

asked Mum, as she smoothed the pillow and gave Kitty a kiss.

Kitty didn't say anything. She was already asleep.

I don't want to
Say Yes

Kitty had one favourite word, and it was "No".

When Mum asked her if she wanted to come shopping, she said "No".

When her brother asked if she wanted him to build her a little house of bricks, she said "No".

When Dad asked her to show him the picture she had painted, or even just to sit on his knee, she always said "No". Just to be awkward. It wasn't that she didn't like shopping, or playing with Daniel, or being nice to Dad. It was just that she hated to say "Yes".

If she didn't say "No", she used her other favourite words, which were "Shan't" and "Won't".

"Oh dear, Kitty," said Mum, "why don't you ever say 'Yes'? Don't you want to be a pleasant, helpful little girl?"

"No!" said Kitty.

One day Kitty was playing in the garden with Dan, when it began to rain.

"Come inside!" Mum called, and Dan went in right away.

But of course, Kitty shouted "No", and rode her red bicycle all the way down the path, shaking the rain out of her hair, and enjoying herself. It rained even harder, making pattering noises in

the trees, and Kitty decided that she liked being alone in the garden, where there was no one to tell her what to do.

But soon she grew tired of playing in the rain, and anyway, she did not like the swishing noise in the trees, and being alone was boring. So she walked into the house very slowly, and made puddles on the kitchen floor. Mum sighed.

"Look at you, you're soaking wet. You'll catch cold unless we change your clothes."

"Shan't," said Kitty.

"Are you going to come, or do I have to make you?" said Mum with a frown.

"No," said Kitty, and ran ahead up the stairs.

In the bedroom Mum pushed and pulled Kitty into dry clothes. Then she told Kitty that she would have to stay in her room until tea, to see if she could learn how to say "Yes", just for a change.

Kitty asked her bears if they liked her – but they didn't say "Yes". She asked her bricks if they liked her – but they all fell down. She asked her books how to say "Yes" – but all their words were locked inside them. Kitty scowled, but still tried hard, and yet the only word that came from her mouth was a very angry "No!"

When Mum called her, Kitty ate her

tea without saying anything, because she knew the wrong word would come out. But when Dan teased her and asked if she had lost her tongue, Kitty kicked him under the table and shouted, "No!"

Kitty felt cross with everyone, and everyone was cross with her. But later Dad sat in the armchair and smiled at the look on her face, calling her a crosspatch.

"It's time to go to bed, Kitty," Mum sighed. "Go and kiss Dad good night."

Kitty stuck out her bottom lip. "No," she said.

"Now I told you to kiss your Dad. You must do as you are told," Mum said, sounding very angry indeed.

"Shan't," said Kitty.

Dad looked up from his newspaper. He knew Kitty very well. He pretended to frown at her, and growled, "Whatever you do, Kitty, I don't want you to kiss me. You mustn't be a good girl, and most of all you mustn't ever say 'Yes', or I will turn into a terrible

monster. Now remember – you *don't* want to kiss me good night, do you?"

Kitty smiled for the first time.

And she called out, "Yes!"

I don't want to
Share

Kitty heard the bad news at breakfast. It was very bad news indeed. But Mum was looking really happy.

"Melissa is coming to play," she said.

"Oh no!" said Kitty.

"Oh no!" said Dan.

Melissa was their cousin, but they didn't like her.

"Melissa's boring," Kitty said.

"Melissa's silly," said Dan, "but at least *I* won't have to play with her. She's your age, Kitty, so you'll have to share all your toys!"

Kitty was cross all day, and wouldn't change out of her dungarees or comb her hair.

At four o'clock the doorbell rang. There on the step stood Auntie Susan and Melissa. Melissa was wearing a pink and blue flowered dress with a white collar, white shoes and socks, and pink and white checked bows in her curly fair hair. She held up her face nicely so that Kitty's mum could kiss it. Kitty hung back and scowled.

"Why don't you take Melissa upstairs to your room, and play until it's time for tea," said Mum firmly. "You can show her the lovely castle you got for your birthday."

"But it's *my* castle," said Kitty. "It's my best toy."

"Sweetie, your cousin's come to see you, and you know we *all* have to share our things," said Mum.

Kitty thought that Mum didn't have to share her typewriter or her dressing table with anyone else, but she just muttered, "I don't *want* to share."

Upstairs in the bedroom, Melissa glanced at the castle and all the little knights on their horses, and tossed her

head. "I don't like that anyway. It's a
BOY's toy," she said.

"Good. So what do you want to do
then?" Kitty asked.

"I want to play dolls."

Kitty ran into Dan's room and brought back Action Man with his army uniform on. "Here's a doll," she said.

Melissa looked horrified. "Dolls aren't like that. Dolls are pretty," she said.

Kitty stared at her and said nothing.

"Haven't you got a dollies' tea set?" asked Melissa at last.

Kitty rummaged in her cupboard and pulled out the old cracked plate she used for mixing paints, a chipped enamel mug, and the battered tin camping dish she had bought for 1p at a jumble sale. "Here you are!" she said.

"Ugh, horrible dirty old things," said Melissa, turning away.

Then Kitty showed Melissa a white plastic football, a box of very messy finger paints, the two broken tractors Dan did not want any more, and a large ball of plasticine Kitty had mixed so

often that all the colours had merged into a dirty grey. "Here you are. You can share all my favourite toys, Melissa," she smiled.

Her cousin stamped her foot. "At home I've got a doll's house, two white fluffy rabbits, some Fuzzy Felt sets, and a tea set with blue roses on it," she said. "And I've got my very own toy make-up set. My toys are much nicer than your toys."

Kitty had a good idea. "Sit in that chair and close your eyes, and I'll make you look like a princess," she said.

Melissa did as she was told, and Kitty took a litle box of face paint sticks from her top drawer.

First she put big circles of bright red on Melissa's cheeks and nose. "Ladies call that blusher," said Melissa.

Then she coloured Melissa's lips dark brown, with a silver outline, with a red line going down to her chin from each corner of her mouth, like teeth. "Ladies call that lipstick," said Kitty.

Then she coloured the space between Melissa's eyes and eyebrows bright green, with black lines running out from the corners of her eyes towards her ears, and black lines underneath. "Ladies call that eyeshadow," said Melissa.

Then Kitty drew a very thick line of

orange over Melissa's eyebrows. "Eye-
brow pencil," said Melissa.

"Now," said Kitty, "you just need
some powder to finish you off. I'll share
Mum's new talc with you." And she
dashed to the bathroom and brought it
back, shaking it into her hand and
patting it over Melissa's face and hair
until it spread in a white cloud all round
them.

Just then Mum and Auntie Susan came upstairs.

"Isn't it nice they are playing so well together?" Mum was whispering as she opened the door into Kitty's bedroom.

Melissa opened her eyes. "Do I look as pretty as a princess?" she asked.

Auntie Susan opened her mouth with horror, but Mum began to laugh.

"Oh Kitty-Kat, what game have you been playing?"

Kitty looked at them both and smiled her sweetest smile. "I was sharing my Monster Mask set with Melissa!" she said.

I don't want to
Tidy my Room

One Saturday morning Kitty was just doing a difficult bit of colouring-in – one of those fiddly shapes where you have to be really careful – when her bedroom door opened with a bang. Dad looked in. "Kitty," he said, "your room is a terrible mess!" He said it very loudly.

Kitty jumped, and her crayon went over the line. "Look what you've made me do!" she shouted. "It's spoilt now!"

Dad took no notice. "Your mum and I have enough to do. You're old enough to learn to put things away," he said, and closed the door again.

Kitty sat at her table, resting her chin on her hands. She wondered why it is that grown-ups always interrupt

children, but if children interrupt grown-ups they are told off. It's always "Wait till I've finished dear", or "Can't you see I'm busy", or "Later", and they carry on just as before.

"Why do *we* have to do as we're told right away?" thought Kitty glumly. "It isn't fair."

But Kitty knew her room *was* in a

mess. She had spread the duvet on the floor to see what it looked like as a rug, and pulled all the toys out of the cupboard to look for her crayons, and rummaged in her drawers to look for a tee-shirt, and put her toy castle on the floor by the bed to see if the teddies would fit into it – which, of course, they wouldn't.

Her pyjamas were on the chair, and a half-eaten biscuit was on the bed.... even Kitty could see Dad's point. "But I don't *want* to tidy my room, and I *won't*," she said.

She tried to go on with her colouring, but the red crayon broke, and Kitty did not know where her sharpener was. She sighed. Walking across the room to look for it, she tripped over the edge of the duvet and nearly fell on the pile of toys. "Oh, banana-skins!" she said.

Then she felt something hard under her foot and heard a terrible *cerr-akkk*! "Oh no," Kitty thought, and looked down. One of her precious knights lay flattened, his arms snapped off, and his shield broken in two. Kitty bent down to pick him up, feeling very sad. But she didn't cry. She decided to wrap him in one of her best handkerchiefs, and keep him forever.

In the chest of drawers her socks and pants and vests were in such a tumble and a jumble that she couldn't find a handkerchief at all. So she put the knight inside one of her socks, and stepped back – right on top of one of the

roller skates which had fallen from the cupboard.

"Aaaaaaah!" yelled Kitty, as the skate shot her across the room, arms and legs flying. "Ohhhhhhh!" she cried as she hit the bed with a bump, and landed on three teddy bears.

Kitty rubbed her back and looked down. The bears looked squashed and uncomfortable, and looked up at her with their sad brown eyes, until she whispered, "Sorry, bears," and picked them up very gently. She put them

carefully in their usual place at the foot of her bed, and said, "That's better, isn't it?"

And to tell you the truth, it was. Kitty looked round her room and suddenly it didn't seem a nice friendly untidiness but a nasty, messy *mess*.

"You can't find things and you break things and you fall over things and you spoil things," muttered Kitty as she pulled the duvet back on the bed, and stared at the pile of toys. There were old cars and broken dolls and a train with no wheels, and all sorts of things that Mum was always telling her to throw away. But Kitty liked her old toys. They were a part of her life.

Suddenly she had an awful thought. If Mum saw them like this she would be certain to say that some of them could go to the school Jumble Sale. They'd promised to send some old things.

Kitty hid all the toys back inside the cupboard, and put her castle on the table, and the old biscuit in the waste paper basket, and found her sharpener on the floor where it had been hidden under the bears (which is why they had looked so uncomfortable).

When Dad came up later she was quietly colouring her picture. "Kitty-Kat," he said in amazement, "you did it!"

Kitty didn't even look up from her work. "You know I always do as I'm told, Dad," she said.

I don't want to
Play with my
Little Sister

On Sunday mornings Mum and Dad liked to stay in bed. Late. When Kitty ran into their room, they groaned and hid under the bedclothes, and mumbled, "It's too early, Kitty. Go and play in your room."

Kitty always complained, and sometimes she cried, and often they let her climb into their bed where it was warm and cuddly. Other times they said "No" very firmly.

One Sunday Mum got very cross because Kitty yelled near her ear. She jumped out of bed, grabbed Kitty by the hand, and pulled her quickly across the landing – into Daniel's room. He

opened one eye, like a sleepy monster.
"Now Dan," said Mum, "we want a
rest today, just for another half hour.
You must look after your little sister."

Daniel frowned and sat up. "I don't
want to play with my little sister," he
said. But it was too late. Mum had gone
back to bed.

Dan looked at Kitty, and Kitty
looked at Dan, and she put out her

tongue. "You've got to play with me, so there!" she said. Daniel buried his head right under his pillow and pretended to snore. "Let's play going to sleep," he said in a muffled voice.

Kitty thought hard. She was so used to *not* wanting to do things, but now she really did – *so much* – want to play with her brother. She remembered something Mum had said to her one day. "Kitty," she said, "you will just have to learn that if you want people to be nice to you, you'd better be nice to them."

Kitty pulled very gently at Dan's pillow and called to him in her nicest, sweetest voice. "Please, Danny, please. If you play with me I'll be your best friend. You're the best big brother in the world." Then she waited.

It didn't work. Dan kept his head under the pillow and said, "Oh go away, Kitty."

Kitty leaned forward. "All right,"

she whispered, "I will go away. But I'll go right back to Mum, and I'LL TELL!"

Dan's face appeared. "You wouldn't."

"I would," said Kitty.

"You wouldn't," said Dan.

"I jolly well would," said Kitty.

"You're a tell-tale," said Dan.

"And you're my brother and you're supposed to play with me," Kitty said.

She waited once more. Dan was very

quiet. "OK," he said at last in a grumpy voice. "What do you want to play then?"

"Let's play a make-believe game," said Kitty excitedly. "Let's pretend we're both farmers and it's a very bad winter and there's a snowstorm and your pillow is a big mountain of snow and we have to drive the tractors over it to rescue the sheep who are buried under it. . . ."

"Hey, stop," said Dan, "you talk too much."

"Well, what do you want me to do?" Kitty asked.

"Help me get the farm stuff out," said Dan, pulling on his dressing gown.

An hour later Mum and Dad woke up again.

"It's very quiet," said Dad.

Mum nodded. "I can't believe the children are actually playing together," she said. "Let's creep along and look."

They tiptoed across the landing and

stood outside the open door of Daniel's room.

Kitty and Dan were crawling around on their hands and knees pushing toy tractors. Kitty had spread out her blue tee-shirt for a pond and put the little ducks on it, and her green tee-shirt made a field for the sheep. A brown cushion made a mountain, and her yellow scarf was a long winding road for the tractors and trailers. As they played she kept on talking . . . and talking . . .

"It was very bad weather after the harvest, and so your tractor slipped into a ditch because of the mud, and we had to get the Landrover to pull it out. So then the ambulance came to take the driver to hospital, and so I had to do all his work. And it's nearly Christmas now, so we'll have to go and cut down this fir tree over here for a Christmas tree in the farmhouse, but before that . . ."

Dan was saying, "We'd better get the

I can't find it!

Contents

I can't find
my Shoe

Kitty was always losing things. It wasn't that she was careless. Of course not. What happened was this. Things she put away very, very carefully just – sort of – moved, all by themselves. And then she got into trouble. It wasn't fair at all.

One morning Kitty was getting ready for school. She found her vest and pants – under the bed. She found her school dress – in the toy box. She found her cardigan – wrapped round one of her teddies. She found her clean socks in the drawer – which surprised her, because that was were they should be.

One shoe was inside Kitty's bed. She knew it must have hopped there itself, because she remembered putting both shoes neatly by her bed the night before.

Kitty's Mum came into the room. She was looking for her watch. 'Oh, hurry up, Kitty,' she said. 'Why do you always have to be so slow in the morning? Now – where's your other shoe?'

'I can't find it,' Kitty said, in a rather muffled voice, because her head was under the quilt.

'What are you doing in there?' Mum asked her.

'Looking for the shoe, of course,' said Kitty.

'Why would it be in bed, you silly thing?'

'Because that's where the other one walked to,' Kitty said, pulling her head out. She frowned at her mother for not understanding.

Kitty's Mum looked all round the room, then sighed.

'You'll just have to go to school in your old trainers.'

'But I'll get into trouble,' said Kitty.

'Well, I'm afraid that will teach you not to lose things,' said Mum, gently.

At breakfast Kitty was so quiet that even Dad noticed. Usually she talked to him while he was reading the newspaper, and he said, 'Um' and 'Ah', even though he wasn't really listening. Today it seemed very quiet, so he looked up and asked what was the matter.

'She's lost a shoe,' said Daniel, munching his toast.

'As usual,' said Mum.

'And I've just remembered something else,' said Kitty unhappily.

'What's that?' asked Dad.

'I don't know where my satchel is either.'

Mum groaned. 'Oh no! What am I going to do with you?'

Kitty jumped up and looked all

round the kitchen, even in the fridge – which made Daniel laugh. 'As if your satchel would be in there!'

'Nothing would surprise me,' said Dad.

Mum was thinking hard. 'You can always find things if you remember what you were doing when you last had them,' she said, 'so what did you do when you came home from school last night?'

Kitty thought, and ran out of the room. Suddenly, she knew what had happened.

When she had come home from school she had wanted to watch children's television, but her teacher had given them some spellings to learn. Not easy ones. Hard ones. Kitty thought that if her Mum saw the spelling book inside her satchel she wouldn't let her watch television.

She remembered that one of the words they had to learn was 'Table', so she had hidden the satchel under the table on the landing – which had a long lace cloth on it, right down to the ground.

Kitty ran upstairs, and looked underneath the cloth. Sure enough, there was the satchel. Quickly, she picked it up and peered inside. And tucked down beside her spelling book, was – the missing shoe. But Kitty hadn't the faintest idea how it had got there.

Mum came up the stairs behind her. 'Kitty!' she said in a cross voice. 'What on earth was your satchel doing underneath that table?'

Kitty didn't answer. Instead she just pulled out the shoe, and held it up in the air with a smile. 'Mum,' she said, 'I think I'm really clever. If I hadn't lost my satchel, I wouldn't ever have found my shoe!'

'You always win, Kitty,' said Mum.

I can't find
my Teddy

There were lots of teddies on the shelf in Kitty's room, and she liked them all very much indeed. But one of them was special. Very special. He was the oldest of the teddies, and his fur was very worn. Daniel had been given him when he was born, but now he lived with Kitty because Daniel said he was too old for teddy bears. The old bear was small, with a squashy nose, and two pink paws, and sparkling brown glass eyes. Kitty called him Mr Tubs, because of his fat tummy. She liked him best of all because he had a lovely old, warm smell that made her feel at home. He smelt of lots of hugs.

One night, in winter, Kitty was getting ready for bed. At first, she couldn't find her pyjamas, but Mum said she should look under the bed first. And of course they were there.

Kitty washed her face and cleaned her teeth without making too much fuss, then ran into Dan's room to say goodnight. Although Dan was older than Kitty he was already in bed, because he had been off school all day with a bad cold. He looked at her sleepily over the bedclothes.

'Goo-ni,' he mumbled, sniffing.

'Goodnight Daniel,' Kitty said. Secretly she liked it when her brother was a bit sick – not because she was mean, but because he seemed younger, and she could be kind to him. When Kitty was ill, Daniel was nice to her too. Brothers and sisters are like that.

Kitty went into her own room, where her Mum was waiting. 'Now, have you got your book, Kitty?' she asked. Kitty looked around – and found the book on the floor under her desk, making a garage for a toy car. Then she jumped into bed at last . . .

'Oh no!' she shouted.

'What's the matter?' Mum asked.

'Where's Mr Tubs? He was in here this morning.'

Mum sighed. 'Kitty – you're *always* losing things,' she said. 'And I thought you loved your teddy too!'

'I do love him,' Kitty almost shouted.

'Then why have you lost him?' asked Mum.

Kitty didn't hear. She was burrowing down under the quilt like a little mole. So many things always hid themselves there . . . But at last her head came out of the bottom. 'He isn't in there,' she said.

They looked under the bed. They peered beneath the chest of drawers. They searched the cupboard. They emptied the laundry basket. And they pulled all the other soft toys off their shelf, just in case Mr Tubs was hiding behind them. But there was no sign of the teddy.

Just then, Dad came into the room. 'What's the matter, Kit?' he asked.

'I can't find my teddy,' she wailed.

'Never mind, we'll find him tomorrow,' Dad said.

That made Kitty cross. 'You KNOW I can't sleep without him. You KNOW I can't!' she shouted.

'Well, we'll just have to find him then,' said Mum.

When Mum had walked all over the house, looking for Mr Tubs, and Dad had been out to the garage to see if he was in the car, and Kitty had even pulled everything out of the airing cupboard – they all met again on the landing.

'Oh no,' sighed Mum, looking at the jumble of clean clothes on the floor.

'Oh no,' groaned Dad, looking at his watch and remembering he was missing a good programme on the television.

'Oh nooooo,' cried Kitty, thinking of poor Mr Tubs.

Then Dad had an idea. 'Where would Mr Tubs *want* to be?' he asked.

Kitty thought, 'In bed with me,' she said.

'Yes, but *why?*'

'Because he's kind and he's cuddly, of course.'

'Mmmmm, I wonder . . . ?' said Mum, thoughtfully, looking quickly towards the door of Daniel's room.

Kitty ran in. She could hear her brother breathing like a very puffy train. She tiptoed to the bed, and prodded all the humps and bumps carefully. What was that . . . ? A stubby paw? A fat round tummy? A funny squashy nose?

She slid her hand beneath the bedclothes, and felt about and . . . pulled out Mr Tubs. He was all warm, and he smelt *wonderful*. 'Hallo, Mr Tubs,' she whispered. 'Did my horrid old brother steal you away?'

Mum and Dad had followed her into the room. They smiled down at Daniel, and at Kitty and the teddy.

'Daniel didn't steal him,' whispered
Mum, 'I think he just wanted some comfort
– don't you?'

'Because when you're ill, you want something to hug – even if you're big,' said Dad.

Kitty nodded. She looked from Mr Tubs
to Daniel and back again. Mr Tubs looked
very happy. 'What will Dan think if he
wakes up and finds him gone?' she asked,
slowly.

'He'll be sad and think, "I can't find my teddy", and *you* know how sad that is,' said Mum.

'Well, do you think I should leave Mr Tubs with Daniel, just for tonight?' said Kitty, feeling very grown-up.

'Yes, I think you should,' said Mum, smiling at Kitty.

And so she did.

I can't find
my Pretty Clothes

It was Saturday – Kitty's favourite day. She was looking forward to playing in her room, and making a mess, and running in the garden, and . . . 'Now Kitty,' said Mum, 'It's Melissa's birthday party today. Had you forgotten?'

Kitty groaned out loud. Then she banged her mug on the table. Then she kicked the table leg. Then she folded her arms crossly and frowned.

Daniel laughed, as usual. 'Oh Kitty-witty, must look pretty,' he sang, ducking as she threw a crust across the table at his head.

Mum clapped her hands. 'That's quite enough,' she said sternly. 'It'll be very nice for you to go to your cousin's party.'

'At least I'll get a going-home bag,' said Kitty gloomily.

She remembered the last time Melissa had a party. Two hours before they had to leave Mum had put her in the bath, to scrub her clean – which took quite a long time. She had washed Kitty's hair and tied it back with two blue *ribbons*. Ribbons! In Kitty's hair! Then she had made Kitty put on the brand new pretty dress she had bought specially. It was pale blue with lots of little white flowers all over it, and a white lace collar and cuffs. Clean white shoes and socks finished Kitty's party clothes.

It was terrible.

Mum had put her in front of the mirror. 'There,' she said. 'Don't you look pretty?'

'I look yukky,' growled Kitty, staring at herself.

'Quite right!' laughed Daniel. '*Pretty-pretty Kitty-witty.*'

'OH SHUT UP!' she had shouted.

That was a year ago. So now Kitty thought for a moment and said, 'My dress won't fit me now.'

'Yes, it will,' said Mum. 'I got it out, and measured it. It was a little bit big last year, so this year it's perfect.'

'Oh,' said Kitty, sticking out her lip in a sulk. There was nothing she could do.

Or – was there?

The day passed quickly, and it was soon time. After the bath, Mum folded Kitty in a big warm towel and said, 'Now run into your room and bring your pretty clothes in here. The hair ribbons are on the hanger too . . .'

Kitty went into her room. Then, after a while, she called, 'I can't find my pretty clothes,' trying to sound worried.

Mum came out of the bathroom. 'But I know they were in your wardrobe. I saw them the other day!'

'I didn't,' said Kitty.

Mum looked on the rail, then pulled open

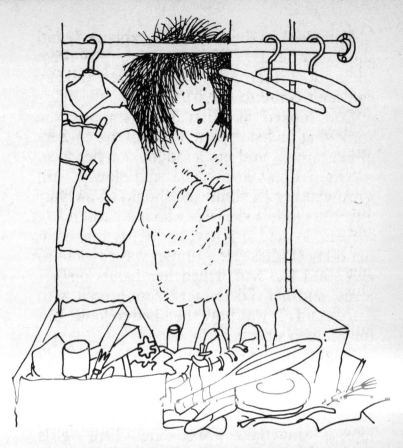

Kitty's drawers. She frowned at the mess.
'Now, where *can* that party dress be?' she
said.

'Oh Mum, I don't know,' said Kitty. 'You
know I'm always losing things.' She crossed
her fingers behind her back, and looked up
at the ceiling.

Just then Dad came into the room.
'What's all the fuss about?' he asked.

Mum looked flustered. She explained, and shook her head. 'That's the only pretty dress she's got. I'll have to ring up Susan and say she can't come to the party.'

Dad looked at Kitty. She stopped the smile that had started to turn up the corners of her mouth, and put a sad look on her face.

'Oh, I don't know,' he said slowly, still staring at her. 'I think she should go anyway – in the clothes she was wearing earlier.'

Mum looked at Kitty, and Kitty looked at her dirty clothes. Her jumper was covered in clay, and she had wiped her hands on her jeans, and her old trainers were brown with dried mud. It was how she liked to look. But for Melissa's party . . .

'Right! In the car now!' said Dad.

Of course, Kitty's cousin Melissa *always* looked pretty, and for her own birthday party she was wearing a dress that looked like a snowflake. Six other little girls gathered behind her at the door, all wearing their best party clothes. They giggled when they saw Kitty. She felt awful.

'My cousin's really *scruffy*,' said Melissa with her nose in the air.

Kitty felt even worse.

After the games, and the tea, and more games, it was time for Dad to come and collect her. Kitty said nothing all the way

home. She didn't even look into her going-home bag to see what was there.

As soon as they reached home, Kitty went upstairs. She crept into the spare room, and opened the door of the bedside cupboard. There, crumpled in a bundle, were her party dress, the blue ribbons, the white socks and the shoes. She took them all back into her own room, and put them in her wardrobe.

She had just finished when Dad came in. 'Do you think you'll ever find your party clothes, Kit?' he asked.

'I expect so,' she mumbled, trying not to look guilty.

'Well,' said Dad, looking wise, 'maybe you couldn't find them today – but you found something else instead, didn't you?'

'What?' Kitty asked.

'You found it's not very nice to look scruffy when people expect you not to – is it?'

'No, Dad,' said Kitty.

'And maybe you'll find you won't tell fibs in the future. Am I right?'

'Yes, Dad,' Kitty said.

I can't find
the Word

It really was not fair, Kitty thought one day, how when you were really cross with someone, and wanted to tell them – all the words disappeared out of your head. That is – all the *good* words. Easy words came rushing into your mind, but they just made you sound babyish. Hard words, really grown-up words, were much harder to find. But they were the ones that would say what you *really* felt. So, when Daniel borrowed her new pencil and lost it, she lost her temper. 'Oh you . . . you . . . you . . . fat pig!' she shouted.

Mum frowned at her over the newspaper. 'Honestly, Kitty. If you're going to be rude to your brother you might as well be rude in an intelligent way.'

'Er . . . what do you mean?' Kitty asked.

'I mean that you might as well call him something that makes sense. Like a . . . a . . . careless robber, or something.'

'I'm not a robber!' yelled Daniel.

'Well, you stole my pencil, didn't you – you . . . you . . . you . . . oooh, I don't know what to call you,' shouted Kitty, running out of the room.

But before she closed the door she heard her brother say, 'Poor Kitty can't find the right word.' He sounded very pleased with himself.

Where do you *find* words? Kitty wondered, lying on her bed. She thought that there might be a sort of box in your mind, a treasure chest full of words, just waiting for you to open it up, and take them out one by one. Then, after a while, you would never have to search for a word. The right one would just jump out of the box, ready to do as you wished. And once that happened, *nobody* would be able to get the better of you, Kitty decided. Not at all. But where do the words come from?

Dad was in his bedroom, listening to the radio. People were talking about politics. There were plenty of words there – all flying out into the air.

Then Kitty wandered downstairs to the sitting room, where there was an enormous bookcase, crammed with books. Plenty of words there too – all locked between the pages. At last she went back into the kitchen, where her mother still sat at the kitchen table, reading the newspaper. That was packed with words too – all dancing about on the large white pages.

Daniel had gone into the garden. So Kitty pulled at Mum's sleeve, and asked, 'Mum – how do *you* find the word you want?'

Mum laughed. 'Sometimes it's hard for grown-ups too,' she said, 'but I know what I do. I read and read and read, and that way I keep putting words into my brain, ready for

when I need them. Like saving up pocket money. A long time – *hundreds* of years ago – they used to call that your own Word-hoard.'

Kitty was excited. 'That's just the way I pictured it!' she said.

'The other thing,' said Mum, 'is not to get cross. When you lose your temper you lose your words as well. People huff and puff, like you do. *That's* no good at all.'

Kitty shook her head. Then Mum got up from the table, and held out her hand to Kitty. 'Come with me,' she said.

They went upstairs again to Daniel's room. Mum searched in his untidy book-

case, until she pulled out a large red book.
'What does that say?' she asked Kitty.

Kitty frowned, and after a little while she
said slowly, 'Jun-ior Dic-shun-erry.'

'That's right,' Mum said. 'Now if you curl
up in a corner with this, you'll find you meet
lots of new words, and some of them might
be very useful!'

Kitty found it hard at first, but soon she
forgot everything. It was such fun to dip into
the book, and read the words (sometimes

that took a little time), and find out what they meant. It was like a new game, and she loved it.

That evening the family sat down together to have supper. Kitty was in a bad mood again, because Daniel had wanted to watch his programme on the television, and Kitty had wanted another one. They quarrelled in the sitting room, and they kicked each other under the table, then Mum burnt her finger on the cooker and she got cross too.

'I haven't got any gravy,' Kitty said in a bossy voice.

'Here – I'll pour some for you,' said Mum.

'I didn't want it *there*, I wanted it *there*, on the potatoes,' Kitty said crossly.

Mum put the jug down, and looked at her. 'Now just stop being so . . . so . . . oh, I don't know the word for what you're being!'

'Aggressive,' Kitty said, pleased. She folded her arms and grinned at her mother. 'You're losing all *your* words now, Mum!'

I can't find
my Courage

Kitty was brave. She never *ever* cried. Or at least, that was what she told her friends at school. Of course, we all cry when we are hurt – even Kitty. And one Saturday, at the swimming pool, she cried a lot.

This is how it happened. Kitty was a good swimmer, and loved to dive into the water. Her Dad always said she was like a little fish. He also told her never to play in a silly way at the swimming pool, because you can get hurt. 'Look at those boys,' he said. 'That's what I mean.'

Some older boys were jumping into the water in a way that made a big splash. They called it 'dive bombs'. It made other people rush to get out of the way. The boys laughed a lot, but Kitty's Dad frowned. 'They're just stupid,' he said.

But Kitty thought it looked fun. She watched for a while. Then she stood on the edge of the pool. Dad and Daniel were in the water. 'Why shouldn't I?' thought Kitty.

SPLASH!

'Owwwwwwwwwwwww!'

It was a horrible feeling. Kitty felt as if the water had jumped up to slap her hard on her arms and legs. When she did her proper dives she slid *through* the water. This time she fell *at* the water – and it hurt.

'Ow-oww-owww-owwww!'

She cried and cried, and Dad cuddled her. He didn't say 'I told you not to do that', or 'Silly girl', or anything like that. He just whispered, 'Poor Kitty-Kat, does it tingle?' and held her close.

'Can we go home now, Daddy?' she asked in a little snuffly voice. Usually she had to be *made* to get out of the water, but Kitty had had enough swimming for one day!

Four days later was the day Kitty went swimming with her class at school. She usually looked forward to it. To be honest, that was because she was one of the best swimmers in the class, and liked showing off – just a little bit.

'Right children, today we're going to do some dives,' said Miss Evans. 'Hands up those who can already dive!'

Kitty put her hand up.

'All right then, Kitty, you can show us,' said Miss Evans with a smile.

Kitty stepped to the edge of the pool. She looked down. The water blinked and flashed at her. It looked fierce. It looked as though it might hit her again, and make her arms and legs tingle.

'Come on, Kitty!' called her friends.

She waited, with her arms stretched out. But she could not dive in.

Miss Evans was jolly and kind, and could see that something was wrong. So quickly she told the class to get into the water and practise their swimming. Then she came up to Kitty. 'What's the matter, Kitty?' she asked.

'I . . . I . . .' Kitty stammered.

'Yes?'

'I can't . . . find my . . . courage,' said Kitty in a small voice.

She told Miss Evans what had happened on Saturday. Miss Evans nodded. 'What we say is, you've lost your nerve,' she said, 'so now you must find it again, Kitty.'

'But *where* do I look for it?' asked Kitty.

'Where you last had it, of course!' said Miss Evans. 'Listen, when you fall off a horse, or a bike, it's very important to get back on again – right away. On Saturday you should have done a proper dive as soon as you stopped hurting. That way you find your courage exactly where you lost it.'

'Oh,' said Kitty. 'So I have to look for it in *there*.' And she pointed to the water.

'Yes,' said Miss Evans, taking her hand and standing on the edge of the pool. 'And I'm going to help you look. Shall we dive in together?'

'I'm afraid the water will hit me again,' Kitty said.

Miss Evans shook her head. 'It won't hurt you if you're kind to it! If *you* don't hit *it*! You see? Trust me.'

Kitty nodded.

'Get ready,' said Miss Evans, 'and go when I count to three.'

Kitty took a deep breath. She stretched out her arms, and bent her knees, and waited.

'One . . . two . . . THREE!'

It was a lovely feeling. The cool water rushed past her ears – and in a second she was up again. Miss Evans' head bobbed next to hers. She smiled. 'And how did that feel, Kitty?' she asked.

101

Instead of answering, Kitty ducked her head forward and did something Daniel had taught her on Saturday, before her awful jump. It was a handstand under water.

She came up shaking the water out of her eyes, and laughing.

'And what were you doing down there?' Miss Evans smiled.

'I was finding some *more* courage at the bottom of the pool,' Kitty panted, 'so now I'll never lose it again!'

I can't find
my Way

It was a lovely summer Sunday, and Kitty woke up early. The birds were singing in the garden. The sun shone through the curtains on Mr Tub's twinkling glass eyes. She could hear Mum and Dad moving around downstairs already.

Kitty felt excited. They were going on a picnic today. There was a beautiful old house, a really big one, in the countryside near them, and you could pay to visit it. 'We'll have a look at all the lovely things in the house, and then have a picnic in the gardens,' said Mum.

'There's a maze too,' said Dad.

'Oh good. And can we have salad sandwiches?' asked Daniel.

'Do we have to look at the things in the house?' asked Kitty, grumpily.

But that was the night before. Now she felt in a good mood, and jumped up to dress. It was funny, but when she did not have to go to school she could always find her

clothes. So, soon she was having her breakfast – and then it was time to go.

When they reached Barrington Manor,
Kitty gasped. The old house was black and
white with tall chimneys, and little windows
with diamond panes of glass. The gardens
were full of bushes and trees, and places to
hide – and all Kitty wanted to do was play.
But when they parked in the car park, Mum
said to Dad, 'I can't wait to see all that
wonderful old furniture,' and Dad said, 'I
hear there are fine suits of armour.' And
Kitty felt bored at the thought of the house.

'I don't want to look at silly old furniture,' she said, stamping her foot.

'Come on, Kitty-Kat,' said Dad, taking hold of her hand, 'it'll be really interesting, you see.'

As they walked along the path to the house, Kitty saw a sign saying, 'To the maze'. She pulled her father's hand. 'Let's just go and look at it, just for a minute,' she pleaded, and he agreed.

When they reached the maze, all Kitty could see were hedges. It didn't look very exciting, or very difficult. Mum said, 'Come *on*! I want to look at the house', and then Kitty did a very naughty thing indeed. She pulled her hand out of Dad's, and ran into the maze. 'Can't catch me', she called over her shoulder.

She ran down a little path, with a wall of hedge each side, and turned a corner, then another corner. She could hear Daniel calling, 'Kitty – come back!' and Mum telling her not to be so naughty.

'I'll just hide for a few minutes and then go back,' Kitty thought, skipping a bit further along the path, then turning another way, and then another. 'Come and find me!' she shouted, but her voice sounded small – muffled by the high hedges. 'You can't find me!' she shouted again – but a bird sang

loudly somewhere near her, and she suddenly couldn't hear her parents at all.

'I think I'll go back now,' Kitty said to herself, turning back the way she had come. But there were two ways to go – which was the right one? She chose one path, but then it turned off sharply towards the middle of the maze. Or was that the way out? She didn't know. It all looked the same.

Kitty remembered Hansel and Gretel in the wood, and wished she had dropped something so that she could find her way out. Or left Dad holding a long thread . . . But it was no good thinking that. She must be brave, and find the right path somehow.

'Daddy!' she called, and thought she heard his voice say 'Hallo'. But it seemed a long way away. Kitty started to walk more quickly. Then she began to run, on and on, further and further, round and round – until she felt quite dizzy. And she felt tears come into her eyes.

At last, turning a corner, she went *crash* – into someone coming towards her. It was a young woman wearing jeans, with long dark hair and a headband round it. She had a kind, suntanned face, and was carrying a pair of garden shears. 'Hallo,' she said, looking at Kitty's face. 'What's the matter?'

Kitty sniffed, 'I . . . can't . . . find . . .

my . . . way.'

The girl smiled, 'Well, you're lucky. I'm Sally, one of the gardeners, and I know the way out. Come on.' And she took Kitty's hand, turned her round, and started slowly to take her out of the maze.

As they walked she told Kitty wonderful stories about Barrington Manor, and how there was a friendly lady ghost who lived in the blue bedroom, and how if you shouted in one corridor you would hear two echoes, and how the maze was built in the days when ladies wore huge white ruffs right up to their ears, and you could see dresses like that in the house . . .

At last they reached the entrance, where Mum and Dad and Daniel were standing, looking a bit worried. 'Oh, *there* you are,' called Mum. 'Dad was just going to find someone to help us.'

'Well, *I* found someone,' said Kitty happily, looking up at Sally. 'I couldn't find my way, and I got a bit scared, but then I found Sally, and she's a gardener, and she works here, and she's been telling me all sorts of things, and can we go and see the house now, Mum?'

Mum laughed. 'Phew,' she said. 'Kitty, I'm a-*mazed*!'

I can't find
my List

Kitty's Mum stood in the kitchen and folded her arms. 'If you say "I can't find it" one more time,' she said, 'I'll *scream*.'

Kitty wasn't listening. She was rummaging in the toy box, throwing things all over the floor. At last she sat back and said, 'I can't find one of my roller skates.'

Daniel grinned. 'Go on then Mum,' he said, 'SCREAM.'

110

And she did.

'Whatever's going on?' asked Dad, coming into the room.

Mum said nothing, so Daniel explained. 'Well, first of all Kitty lost her toothbrush. Then she couldn't find her sandals. Then she lost her pocket money, which Mum had only just given to her. Then she started to eat a biscuit and put it down somewhere and couldn't find the bit that was left. Then she lost Mum's purse, when Mum asked her to fetch it so she could give her more pocket money. And then she couldn't find . . .'

Kitty scowled. 'Tell-tale,' she said.

'No, he's not,' said Dad. 'I asked, and he told me, that's all. He's not trying to get you into trouble, are you, Dan?'

Daniel hid his grin. 'No,' he said, looking very good.

They all looked at Kitty, and she looked back at them. Then her mouth turned down at the corners. It wasn't fair, she thought. Everybody was against her. And it wasn't her fault that she lost things. It was so exciting to rush from one game to another, and there was so much to think about, you couldn't remember things. It wasn't her fault.

'Why doesn't Daniel forget things and lose things?' she asked, quietly.

'Because I'm clever,' he said, in an important voice.

Kitty's mouth turned down even more, and Mum felt sorry for her. 'It's got nothing to do with being clever,' she said. And she took Kitty on her knee, whilst Dad started to make a salad for lunch. 'Let's talk about it, Kit,' she said, 'and see what we can do about it. Now – *why* do you lose things?'

'Because I forget where they are,' said Kitty, 'I forget to remember where I put them.'

'Is it because your room's a mess?' asked Mum, gently.

'Yes,' said Kitty.

'Well, I know what the answer is,' said Dad, shaking lettuce leaves in the sink. 'Organisation!'

'What?' Kitty asked.

'Or-gan-is-a-tion,' he said again. 'It means a tidy mind. It means a tidy room. It means making lists.'

'What sort of lists?' asked Kitty.

'Well, you should have a list of all the things you need to take to school, and then you wouldn't lose them.'

To be truthful, Kitty couldn't quite see why this would work. But she liked the idea. It sounded fun. 'I'll get a notebook and pencil,' she said, rushing to the sideboard. But after a few moments she came back. 'I can't

112

find a pencil,' she said.

'Right, that's it,' said Mum. 'We'll start
by having your room tidied today – so that
you know that pencils are in one drawer in
your desk, notebooks in another, and plasticine in another. It will make life much

easier. And you can make a list of all the
things, and a list of everything you need to
take to school, so that each night you can get
them all ready. And then you won't lose
things.'

'It's a brilliant idea,' said Dad.

All afternoon Kitty worked. Mum came to
help her. The clothes were put in the right
drawers in little piles, all Kitty's toys were
sorted out on different shelves in her cupboard, and all her art stuff was arranged in
the different places in her little desk. Even
the teddies were put tidily on their shelf,
although Mr Tubs didn't look as if he liked
it.

As she did it, Kitty made a little list in her
notebook. It said things like, 'Monday. Art

Club. Apron in Bottom Drawer', and so on. Except that sometimes she spelt the words wrongly.

At last it was all finished. Kitty was proud of her list, and showed everyone. Then she went out into the garden to play for a while. She swung on the swing, and she rode her bicycle, and she chased butterflies. Then Daniel suggested they play a game of hide and seek all over the house until it was time for bed.

'Oh, I wish it wasn't school tomorrow,' said Kitty, when she had had her bath.

'Nonsense,' said Mum, 'because now you're like a new girl. Now you're an organised girl, aren't you?'

Kitty nodded. It was true. Everything was going to be different now. 'Good girl,' said Mum. 'Now you go into your bedroom, and get all your things ready for me to see. And in the morning we'll have a nice peaceful time instead of the usual rush.'

Kitty went into her room. It looked horrid, she thought, all neat – like a room nobody lived in. Now . . . time to get everything ready . . .

Oh dear. She looked in the pocket of the dirty jeans she had been wearing, and then in her jacket in the wardrobe, and then underneath the teddies, and then in her desk drawers, and then amongst her clothes. But it was nowhere to be found.

After a while Kitty's Mum and Dad came into the room. 'Now look,' her mother was saying, 'she's been such a good . . . OH NO!'

The room looked as if a whirlwind had swept it up into the air and then dropped it again. Kitty was kneeling and rummaging in the bottom of her wardrobe. She stuck her head out cheerfully, and said, 'Guess what? I can't find my list. That must make it a lost list!'

'Oh, *Kitty*!' was all they could say.

I can't find
the Car Keys

It was Saturday morning in Kitty's house. Mum was taking Dad to the dentist, then taking Kitty and Daniel shopping, and then they were going to the swimming baths. Kitty didn't like the shopping much, but she wanted to go swimming, and so she said nothing. Anyway, Mum had said she might buy her a new drawing book.

For once she was ready on time. She had her anorak on, and her swimming costume wrapped in her towel under her arm – and waited by the front door. Daniel came down next. He looked surprised to see Kitty there before him, and stood with her.

'Where's Mum?' asked Kitty.

'Getting ready,' said Dan. 'You know how long she takes!'

Dad came out of the sitting room and stood with them. After a while he looked at his watch and shouted up the stairs. 'Hurry up, love! The children are all ready!'

After a while Kitty's Mum came running

118

down the stairs looking worried. She went into the kitchen, and came out. She went into the sitting room, and came out. Then she went upstairs again.

'What are you looking for?' asked Dad.

'I can't find the car keys,' she called.

Dad groaned. 'Oh no,' he said, 'I'll be late for my appointment.'

Kitty's Mum came down again, and

emptied her handbag on the hall table. Kitty stared. It was such a messy pile of papers and tissues and bottles of scent and make-up and bus tickets and pens and pencils and half-finished rolls of sweets . . . . 'Yuk,' said Kitty.

'Messy Mum,' grinned Daniel.

'That's not helpful,' she said crossly.

Dad searched behind all the cushions in the sitting room, and looked on the mantle-piece. Daniel walked up and down the garden path to see if she might have dropped them. Mum ran all over the house, getting more and more bad-tempered. 'Oh, where can they be?' she said.

Now Dad was a bit cross too. 'Can't you remember where you had them last?' he asked.

'In the car! I must have left them in the car!' she said, looking cheerful.

But Dad came in from the garage with empty hands. 'Not there – I do wish you wouldn't lose things,' he said.

'I *don't* lose things – I've only lost the car keys,' said Mum, sounding crosser than ever.

'You always tell me off for losing things, Mum,' Kitty piped up.

'And that's NOT helpful either,' said Mum.

'Better keep out of the way, Kit,' said Daniel, going upstairs to his room.

But Kitty thought and thought. She *was* always getting into trouble for losing things, but that had taught her something. She was sure she could find the car keys, and then Mum and Dad would stop being cross, and then the day would be saved. She *hated* it when her Mum and Dad were angry with each other. She would do anything to stop it.

So she thought even harder. Now . . . when did Mum last use the car?

Yesterday.

But *when* yesterday?

When she had to take that pile of jumble down to the church hall, ready for the sale.

So – what was she wearing?

The answer shone in Kitty's mind like a ray of sunlight.

Kitty's Mum usually wore a comfortable old blue jacket that hung by the kitchen door. She had already looked in its pockets for the car keys.

But Kitty remembered her Mum saying she would probably meet Mrs Briggs at the hall, who was in charge of the jumble sale. Mrs Briggs talked in a funny voice and was rather rich, and bossy, and always wore a coat with a fur collar. Kitty didn't like her much because she always patted her and said, 'And how are we today?', as if she was about two.

For some reason, Mrs Briggs made Kitty's Mum feel nervous. So if she knew she was going to meet her, she wouldn't want to look scruffy . . .

Quickly Kitty ran upstairs. She went into her parents' bedroom, and pulled open the wardrobe door. There was Mum's new purple coat on its hanger, looking funny with its padded shoulders. Kitty put her hand in one pocket. Nothing there. Then in the other pocket . . . and of course there was a jingling sound.

When she came downstairs Dad was standing by the phone. 'It's no good,' he was saying, 'I'll just have to ring up and tell the dentist I'm not coming.'

'Oh, I'm sorry, dear,' said Kitty's Mum, unhappily.

'No, you won't!' called Kitty, coming down the stairs like someone in a play and holding the car keys above her head. 'Just look what *I've* found!'

Dad picked her up and swung her about, just as he used to do when she was very small. Then, when she was on the ground again, Mum knelt down to give her a hug.

'Kitty, you're such a clever girl. How did you know where to look?'

Kitty explained. 'You always tell me to remember what I was doing when I last had the things I lost, don't you, Mum?' she said.

Mum nodded. 'But I still don't know how you thought of looking in my best coat,' she said slowly.

Dad winked at Kitty. 'That's easy,' he said. 'Your daughter *knows* you. She knows you're a bit afraid of posh people, and a bit proud yourself. I'll tell you what. Kitty's found more than the car keys. She's found you out!'

It's not fair!

Contents

It's not fair!

that I'm Little

Kitty was the smallest girl in her class. Usually she did not care. She could swim well, and run as fast as most people – well, almost – and once came first in the egg and spoon race on Sports Day. So it did not matter – being small. That was what Kitty thought.

But one day something happened to make her change her mind. It was one of those days when nothing went right.

First of all, there was a new boy in Kitty's class. His name was Tom, and he was very, very tall. Kitty didn't like him very much, because he called her 'Shrimp'.

The whole class was working on a mural in paint and cut-out paper, and on this day Kitty and Tom and two other children were chosen to do special extra work on it.

Kitty was very excited. She loved painting – especially when you could be really messy.

That was why she wanted to paint the sky, with lovely big fluffy clouds floating along. But each time she tried Tom laughed at her. 'You can't reach,' he said. 'You're too small.' And he leaned over her head, and did the bit she wanted to do.

At break she found someone had put her

jacket on one of the higher pegs she could not reach, and she wouldn't ask Tom or anyone to get it down. So she went outside without it, and felt cold. Then the playground helper told her off for not wearing a coat.

'I couldn't reach it,' said Kitty, in a small voice.

'Oh, you're such a *dear little* thing,' said the lady, nicely.

Kitty sighed. It really was not fair.

Then it was the games lesson, when the girls had to play netball. They were learning to stop each other getting the ball. You had to dodge quickly, and jump very high. Kitty wasn't very good at that.

Today she was worse than ever. She did not get hold of the ball once. All the other girls had longer arms and legs, and it seemed easy for them. Afterwards one of the girls said something that hurt Kitty very much. 'No one will want you in their team, Kitty. You're too *tiny*!'

Kitty was very quiet when she got home. Her mum noticed. At last Kitty burst into tears. 'It's not fair that I'm little,' she sobbed.

Kitty told her mum everything. Mum nodded. 'It isn't easy. *I* was small when I was a little girl, and you ask Daniel what

Surprised, Kitty went to find her big brother to ask him. He made a face. 'They sometimes call me Shorty,' he said. 'But it's always very friendly, so I don't mind!'

'Are you small too?' asked Kitty.

'Yes. But I'd rather be me than the boy in our class who's so tall and thin they call him Stringy!'

'You see,' said Mum, 'most people have got something about themselves they would like to change. When you know that, it makes you feel better about yourself.'

Kitty thought about that, and she made a plan. The next day, at playtime, she made herself feel brave enough to go up to Tom when he was standing on his own.

'Tom, can I ask you something?' she said.

'What, Shrimp?'

'If you had one wish, what would you change about yourself?'

The tall boy looked surprised. Then he went pink, and whispered, 'My hair. I *hate* my hair.' Kitty looked at it. It was orangey-brown. She thought it was rather nice.

'At my old school they called me Carrots,' he said, 'and it wasn't *fair*. But don't you tell anyone, will you Shrimp?'

Kitty said she wouldn't.

Then she found Susie, the big strong girl who had said Kitty was no good at netball, and asked her the same question. Susie frowned, and answered quickly. 'My size,' she said, 'because I feel like an elephant. I'd like to be smaller. I'd like to be like *you*.'

'Like me?' squeaked Kitty, amazed.

Susie nodded.

Kitty looked round the playground, at all the children running around. Some tall, some small. Some fat, some thin. Some dark, some fair. Some shy, some bold. Some

who could sing, some who could swim.
Some dainty, some clumsy . . .

'We're *all* different,' she said to herself,
'and I suppose *that's* fair!'

It's not fair!

that People Can't Take a Joke

'Kitty! You're the naughtiest child in England!' said Mum.

'How do you know? You haven't met them all,' said Kitty.

'Oh, very clever,' said Mum, in her irritated voice.

'Thanks, Mum!' said Kitty.

Her mother opened her mouth – then closed it again. Kitty thought she looked like a fish, and said so. It made her laugh. Then

Mum got up from the table, and started to come towards her – so Kitty thought it was time to leave the room.

She ran into the hall, and up the stairs, bumping into Dad, who was walking down. He dropped his book with a crash, and it tumbled to the bottom of the stairs, bending its cover back.

'Oh, be careful, Kitty,' he shouted. 'Look where you're going!'

'*You* could see me coming,' retorted Kitty.

'That's not the point,' said Dad.

'Yes it is,' said Kitty, ''cos if *you* don't see, why should *I* look?'

Dad frowned. 'I'm not standing here arguing with you, Kitty,' he said, 'because I think you're a very cheeky little girl.'

And with that he stomped off down the stairs and closed the sitting-room door with a slam.

This time Kitty didn't laugh.

On the landing she met Daniel, her brother, coming out of his room wearing his new glasses. He didn't like his glasses, at all, even though he only really had to wear them for reading.

Kitty giggled.

'Hallo, *Wol*,' she said.

'What?' said Dan, puzzled.

'Wol,' she smiled. 'You know, in the Pooh Bear story – it's how poor old owl spelt his own name. WOL!' She giggled.

Daniel knew what she meant right away, and his face went red. 'I don't look like an owl,' he said, in his crossest voice. 'And even if I did you shouldn't say so. It's nasty.'

Then he rushed past her down the stairs, with angry clattering footsteps.

Kitty was still smiling, but the smile froze on her face. Slowly she walked into her own room, and looked into the mirror. She felt as if everybody in the house was against her.

The trouble with people (she thought) is that they never understand jokes. She wasn't trying to be nasty, or cheeky, or clever. She was only trying to be funny, and that was different.

'It's just not *fair*,' she said to her own frowning reflection. 'None of them can take a joke.'

Then she thought of the way Dad and Dan teased her, and expected her to smile with them . . . And it was then that Kitty had her Great Idea.

An hour later it was time for lunch. She heard Dad calling her name, and she went slowly downstairs, sitting at the table without a word.

Nobody in Kitty's house stayed cross for long, and so Dad smiled at her. 'What have you been doing upstairs, Kit?' he asked.

'Just reading,' she replied, in a polite, flat voice – not at all like her own, 'and tidying my room.'

'Gosh, are you feeling all right?' joked her mother, as she passed the plates.

'Oh yes, I'm fine, thank you,' said Kitty in the same voice.

Daniel looked at her strangely. He had taken his glasses off now, and seemed to have forgotten her joke. 'Do you want to play football after lunch?' he asked.

'No, thank you,' Kitty said quietly. 'I don't want to get dirty.'

All through the meal it was the same. Kitty was quiet and polite – and very, *very* dull. She never once smiled, or laughed, or giggled, or teased, or talked with her mouth full, or any of the things that made her *Kitty*. She said 'yes, please' and 'no, thank you' as if they were strangers and she had to be on her best behaviour.

By the time they had finished the meal, the other three were looking at her with astonishment.

'Are you sure you're not feeling poorly?' asked her mother, sounding really worried.

'You're not my normal little Kit,' said her dad.

'Kitty – you're being really *boring*,' grumbled Dan.

At that, Kitty got to her feet. 'Right!' she said, and folded her arms. 'Listen! When I'm being jokey and teasing you all, you don't like it. Then when I'm quiet and polite and serious you don't like that either. Do you think that's fair?'

'Er – no,' said Dad.

141

'Not really,' said Mum.

Daniel just shook his head.

Kitty was triumphant. 'There you are then,' she said. 'So you have to decide which sort of *me* you want to have around.

It's only fair.'

Dad smiled. 'Oh, I know what I think,' he said, and Mum smiled too, nodding before he had spoken. 'I'd rather have the Kitty who's the funniest girl in the world.'

'How do you know?' grinned Kitty.
''Cos you don't know all the rest!'

It's not fair!

that he Goes
to Bed Late

It happened the same way every evening.
Mum came into the sitting room and tapped
Kitty on the shoulder. 'Time for bed, love,'
she said.

Kitty scowled and pointed to where Dan
was reading, or drawing or watching some
television. 'Tell him, too,' she said.

Mum sighed. 'It's not Daniel's bed-time,'
she said.

'That's not fair,' Kitty wailed. 'He always
stays up later than me.'

'That's because he's older than you are,'
said Mum. 'Honestly, Kitty, I shouldn't
have to say that again.'

And then Kitty gave in, and went upstairs
as slowly as possible, muttering dark things
about her brother and how it wasn't fair that
being older gave you treats – and so on.

But then came a night when the story was
different. Two weeks earlier a new family

had moved in next door, and Kitty was
pleased that amongst their three children
was a boy who was exactly her age. He was
called William. They liked the same games,
and soon found out everything about each
other.

So when Kitty's mother came to send her
to bed Kitty looked up and said, 'It isn't
fair.'

'I don't believe it!' said Mum. 'I've *told* you Dan is older and that's why . . .'

'Ah,' said Kitty. 'I'm not talking about him. I'm talking about William! He goes to bed only half an hour before Daniel does, and William is *exactly my age*.'

'Oh,' said Mum.

There was a short silence.

Kitty was triumphant. 'So I think I should be allowed to stay up as long as William.'

'All families have different rules, Kitty,' said Mum.

'I don't think that's fair,' said Kitty.

'Well, all children need different amounts of sleep,' said Mum, 'and that's got nothing to do with fairness!'

'Some people need to eat less food than others, too,' said Dad, from behind his newspaper.

All that week Kitty kept on. And on. Each night she complained. She asked Dad what he thought, and he agreed with Mum – of course. She asked Daniel – and he was on her side.

She even asked William's mother if she thought it was fair that she had to go to bed earlier than William. Mrs Jones looked embarrassed. 'That's up to your mummy, Kitty,' she said.

At last Kitty's mother could stand it no

longer. She had been busy and by Sunday
night she was tired. So when Kitty started to
say, 'Can't I stay up a little bit longer, as late
as . . .' Mum interrupted.

'ALL RIGHT! We'll do an experiment.
This week you can stay up till Dan's
bed-time, which is later than William's.
That way, he'll start telling *his* mum it's not
fair, which will make a change – and *you* can
see how much sleep you need.'

'Oh, Mum. THANKS,' Kitty gasped.

It was wonderful to stay up late that night – as if it was Christmas or New Year. Kitty felt very grown-up. And the next morning she didn't feel a bit tired. 'You see, I was right,' she said to Mum.

But on Tuesday Kitty had a bad day in school. She lost her pen, and somebody pushed her over in the playground, and she couldn't find her gym shoes, and – oh, lots of little things went wrong.

By the end of the afternoon her head was aching a bit, and she found herself thinking longingly of cuddling up with Mr Tubs in her little white bed. When the friendly clock on the mantelpiece showed her normal bed-time, Kitty nearly got up – then she remembered.

Dad and Mum were watching something boring on the television, and Daniel was doing his homework at the kitchen table.

Kitty stared at the screen, then at her book, but her head ached.

Still she wouldn't give in.

By the time it came to Thursday she felt tired. Very tired. 'Oh, Kitty, you've got dark circles under your eyes,' said her teacher.

'You keep yawning, Kitty,' said William – who looked as fresh as a daisy.

'Why don't *you* yawn?' she asked.

''Cos I'm not tired,' he said cheerfully.

'*Oh, I am!*' thought Kitty. But she didn't say it.

When Saturday morning came, Kitty slept and slept and slept.

She slept through her favourite cartoon programme on the television, which she was always allowed to watch.

She slept right through the cooked breakfast Mum always made on Saturday as a treat.

She slept, even though Dad called her loudly, and so he took Dan to the park for football without her.

By the time she came downstairs almost the whole of lovely Saturday morning had gone. The sun was shining in the garden, Dad and Daniel had gone – and Kitty felt she had missed out.

Mum was setting the table for lunch. She smiled at Kitty gently. 'It's not fair, you know,' she said.

'What's not fair?' Kitty asked.

'Well, what you've been doing is catching up on your sleep, because you simply haven't been giving yourself enough. And I don't think that's a *bit* fair, do you?'

'No,' said Kitty. 'It's not.'

It's not fair!
that we Can't Stay

It was the summer holiday, and the most perfect one ever. Kitty's parents had rented a little cottage in the heart of the country. It wasn't big or grand: a sitting room, a kitchen, two little bedrooms and a bathroom under a thatched roof – that's all. But Kitty loved it.

She and Daniel had to share a room, which normally they hated – but that couldn't spoil their holiday. They hardly ever quarrelled – not *here*.

For two whole weeks she and Daniel ran wild, like little squirrels – climbing trees, playing hide-and-seek in the big garden, going for long walks in the woods with Mum and Dad.

'I've never had such a lovely time,' Kitty said.

But now it was the last day. Dad was sweeping the stone floor of the little kitchen,

and Mum was upstairs, packing their bags. It was over. And Kitty couldn't bear it.

Dad found her sitting by the sitting-room window, looking out across the fields, with a very sulky look on her face.

'Mum's calling you, Kit,' he said. 'You've to go and start packing your toys.'

Kitty said nothing.

'Come on – what's the matter?' asked Dad.

'Donwannagoback – noffair,' she mumbled, without turning round.

Dad laughed. 'What are you complaining about now?'

Kitty swung round to face him, and folded her arms. 'I said it's not fair we can't stay,' she said, crossly. 'I don't want to go back to our boring old house, in the boring old town, and go to boring old school. I want to stay here for ever and ever.'

'But you *can't*, Kit,' said Dad.

'I know – and it's not FAIR!' shouted Kitty, bursting into tears and running out of the room.

An hour later Dad carried the suitcases downstairs, and put them in the car. Daniel was helping. Mum was tidying the sitting room. But there was no sign of Kitty.

'Kitty!' Mum called, sounding worried.

'What's wrong?' asked Dad.

Mum rushed past him, and looked into the downstairs toilet. 'Oh, where *is* that girl?' she said.

They looked everywhere – under the beds, in the bathroom, in the wardrobe, behind the sofa, under the tables, even in the wicker basket on the landing. But there was no sign of Kitty.

Daniel called her name loudly.

'Oh . . . she wouldn't wander off and get

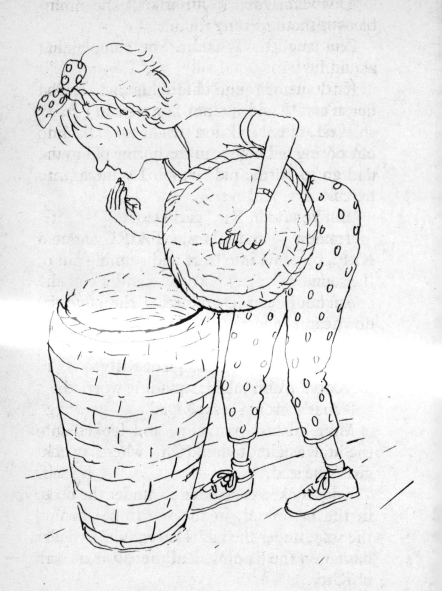

lost, would she?' Mum asked, in a very anxious voice.

'No way,' said Dad. 'She knows that would be wrong and silly, and I *know* she'd never do it. No – she's hiding, that's all. She doesn't want to go home.'

'Well, she's found a really good hiding place,' said Daniel, rather pleased at the thought that his sister was going to get into trouble.

'So how can we get her out of it?' murmured Dad. 'Hmm, maybe I've got a plan . . .'

At that moment Kitty was sitting in the one place they hadn't thought of looking: the little lean-to shed where old deck-chairs were kept. Or at least – Mum had just looked in quickly, peering through the dusty glass in the door. There was a spider's web over a hole in the glass. 'Ugh, Kitty would never go in there,' she thought.

But Kitty hid behind two stacked deck-chairs, feeling very pleased with herself. 'Now they won't be able to go,' she said to herself.

Just then she heard Dad calling. 'We're off now, Kit,' he shouted, 'so if you don't want to come with us, you can stay here.'

'Goodbye,' shouted Mum and Daniel.

'Ha, if they think I'd fall for that one . . .'

smiled Kitty. But then she heard the car doors slam, then the engine start, and then the sound of the car driving away. She waited for a while, not believing what she had heard.

It was quiet.

Very quiet.

Something rustled at the back of the shed, and a spider ran across the floor.

Kitty decided she had been in there long enough.

She crept from her hiding place, and stood listening. Not a sound. The holiday cottage that had been full of family noise was now silent and empty, and Kitty didn't like it. But she knew she had to be brave.

'Right then, I'll go and read my book in the sitting room . . . then I'll go for a walk, then . . .' she said, in a small voice.

It was so *very* quiet.

Slowly she walked up to the back door and pushed it open. It was funny – she had never noticed it creak like that before. In the kitchen the tap went *drip, drip, drip*. It sounded awfully loud in the empty house.

'Oh, dear,' said Kitty. 'I don't think I like it here any more.'

But what was that? Was it a sound. . .?

Slowly she pushed open the door into the little sitting room, and there she saw . . . Mum, Dad and Daniel, sitting on the sofa, grinning at her.

'OH!' cried Kitty, and ran into Mum's arms.

'We knew you'd come out,' said Daniel.

'As if we'd go and leave you,' said Mum.

'We parked the car outside the gate, and crept back,' said Dad.

Kitty was so relieved she didn't say

another word about staying, and Mum and Dad didn't tell her off for hiding.

But two weeks later it was her birthday. And Mum and Dad's present was very big.

Kitty was thrilled to see her very own little playhouse, with a painted thatched roof, and painted roses round the door.

'There you are, Kit,' said Dad. 'Now you've got your very own cottage, to have holidays in all year round!'

It's not fair!
You Always Win!

It was such fun having a new friend next door. Kitty and William got on really well – most of the time. Every Saturday morning one of them would squeeze through the hole in the fence, and soon they would have a good game going.

That is – until they quarrelled. And as they knew each other better they started to quarrel more and more. It wasn't that they liked each other less. It was just that they were too alike. And both of them wanted to win. All the time.

Kitty would often come back from William's house sulking.

'Had one of your tiffs, dear?' Mum would say.

'They're just like an old married couple,' teased Dad – which made Kitty crosser than ever.

But soon she or William would feel bored.

161

So one of them would squeeze through the
hole in the fence – and soon they would be
playing again.

On this particular Saturday it was pouring
with rain. Kitty pulled on her anorak,
picked up a carrier-bag, stuffed it full of
games, told her mum where she was going,
and ran next door.

'What shall we play?' asked William.

'Snakes and ladders,' said Kitty.

But the red counter Kitty chose always
seemed to land on snakes' heads, whilst

William's blue counter climbed up ladder after ladder.

At last – 'I've won!' – he cried.

Kitty said nothing – even when he won the second game as well.

Then they tried Ludo. This time Kitty chose blue for luck, and William swapped to green. But however hard she shook the dice, Kitty kept throwing ones and twos, whilst William threw sixes. The green counters raced around the board, and landed home, whilst the blue counters just couldn't get going.

At last – 'I've won!' – he cried.

Kitty said nothing, but her mouth turned down.

'What about snap?' asked William with a grin.

'Oh, all right,' sighed Kitty.

It was hopeless. William spotted the pairs so quickly, and yelled, 'SNAP!' so loudly – and soon he was sweeping up the pile. Kitty threw down her last card. Her face went red.

'It's not fair!' she shouted. 'You *always* win!'

'That's because I'm clever,' said William with a grin, flicking the pack of cards.

Kitty was so disappointed she wanted to cry.

Just then William's big sister Sally walked

past. She was thirteen, and *very* grown-up, and Kitty thought she was wonderful. Sally liked Kitty too – and she heard what William said.

'That's rubbish, Will,' she said. 'It's got nothing to do with being clever. You're just lucky.'

'No, it's *skill*,' boasted William.

'Doesn't take any skill to throw a dice,' snorted Sally.

'Whatever it is, it's *not fair*,' wailed Kitty.

'Crybaby,' said William.

At that, Sally took hold of Kitty's hand, and led her upstairs without another word. Her room was marvellous; full of beads and books and ornaments, with posters of pop singers and Sally's own bright paintings on the walls.

'Now,' said Sally, taking out a little chess set. 'William's just learning this. Can you play?'

'Dad started to show me, but . . .'

'Right. Now, you remember how each piece moves. . .?'

Kitty remembered, and soon she was absorbed in the game. Sally told her how to work out moves well in advance, and how to guess what the other person would do, and

when to move the King and the Queen. It was such fun – like fitting together the pieces in a jigsaw puzzle. Kitty loved it.

After nearly an hour had passed, Sally said, 'Now you go downstairs and challenge William.'

Kitty did just that.

They played in silence, concentrating really hard. At last William looked up with a frown. 'You're *winning*,' he said – as if he didn't believe it.

'Checkmate!' said Kitty.

'Not fair . . .' William started to moan.

'Too right!' said Kitty. 'It's jolly unfair that *some* of us have all the skill!'

It's not fair!

that Things aren't Fair

It was a cold morning in November, and Kitty and her mum were walking along a busy road. They were going to see Gran, who lived in a special home for old people. Kitty liked visiting Gran. She always had a roll of sweets in her pocket.

Suddenly Kitty heard the sound of music. On the corner of the street stood an old man, playing a mouth organ. His clothes were worn. In front of him, on the pavement, was a battered hat, in which some people had put money.

He didn't play the mouth organ very well, and that made Kitty feel even more sorry for him.

'Mum, can we put some money in his hat?' she whispered.

'Of course,' said Mum, and pulled a silver coin from her pocket. Kitty felt embarrassed as she threw it down, and ran off quickly.

167

'Why is he poor, Mum?' Kitty asked.

'I don't know, love.'

Kitty said nothing.

As they waited to cross the road she noticed a huge poster on the wall opposite. It showed some children who were very, very thin, and was asking people to send money to help those children.

'Do they live in Africa, Mum?' Kitty asked.

Mum nodded. 'Well, *why* haven't they got enough food?' asked Kitty. '*We* have, so why haven't they?'

Mum sighed. 'Oh, I don't really know, Kitty. Sometimes it's because of the weather . . . it's all so complicated.'

Kitty said nothing.

Gran was in a good mood. She sat knitting, and her eyes sparkled when she saw them. 'How's my untidy little girl?' she said, reaching out to ruffle Kitty's hair.

'What are you knitting, Nana?' Kitty asked.

Gran held up a long shapeless-looking jumper. 'It's for your dad,' she said. 'It's his Christmas present.' Kitty imagined Dad wearing it, and giggled.

Soon she was quietly munching sweets, as Mum and Gran talked. But then she noticed that Gran didn't look so cheerful any more.

She was saying that she hadn't been well,
and added, 'Don't worry, it's just old age,
that's all.'

'You're not old, Gran – not *really* old,'
Kitty said.

'Oh yes, I am,' sighed Gran.

Kitty wanted to go home, but felt guilty
for thinking it. Later, when they did leave,
she didn't want to look at all the other old
ladies, waiting for their visitors. It made her
feel sad.

All the way home she said nothing.

When they were sitting at the kitchen table Mum said, 'Come on now, Kit, what's the matter?'

'Why do people have to grow old? I don't want *you* to get old,' Kitty said.

'But I have to,' smiled Mum. 'We all have to.'

'Why can't we just all stay as we are?'

'Because we can't. It's not possible.'

Suddenly Kitty felt angry. She banged the table with her fist, so that all the cups and plates rattled.

'IT'S NOT FAIR!' she shouted.

'What isn't?' asked Mum.

'EVERYTHING. I feel so sorry for people like that poor man in the street, and then I think that we've got so much more than all those people in Africa and India, and I don't know why we haven't all got the same. And then Gran isn't very well, and I know she hates being old and not being able to do things . . . It's just not . . .'

Kitty felt like crying.

'Come on my knee,' said Mum. They had a big cuddle, then she whispered, 'Things do seem very unfair, don't they, love?'

Kitty nodded. 'But *why*, Mum?'

'I can't tell you. There isn't a grown-up in the world who could tell you the answer,' said Mum.

171

'I thought grown-ups knew everything,' sighed Kitty.

Mum shook her head. 'No, love. Oh, I *could* tell you that if we weren't so selfish we could give more to poor people – whether they live here or the other side of the world.

But there's more to it than that. And in any case, that wouldn't stop people being ill or old, would it?'

Kitty shook her head.

'I wish that *everything* was fair,' she said.

'So do I,' said Mum. 'But it can't be.'

'It still makes me cross,' said Kitty.

'And it probably always will,' said Mum.

It's not fair!
She's Got More Presents

Christmas was the best day of the whole year, of course, and this time it seemed better than ever. Kitty's stocking had been crammed with funny little toys and jokes.

And after breakfast, when they opened their main presents, Kitty was so pleased. Mum and Dad had bought her what she most wanted: a huge art set, with lots of different paints, paper of all sizes, felt-tips, crayons, pencils and rubbers – all packed into a lovely carrying case.

She had plenty of books too, because she loved reading, and a lovely long scarf from Gran, in rainbow colours. Dan gave her three more soldiers and horses for her castle. She was very happy.

Kitty and Daniel were sorry about one thing, though.

This year Mum and Dad had arranged to go to have Christmas dinner with Aunty

Susan and Uncle Joe. *That* wasn't so bad, although they said they would rather have their own turkey.

But going to that house meant something that made them both moan.

'*Melissa*,' said Daniel, making a rude face.

'Yuk,' said Kitty.

They had to leave all the lovely clutter of wrapping paper and ribbons and glittery pom-poms, and go out. 'Aunty Susan's house is so *tidy*,' groaned Kitty in the car.

'Just like Melissa. Maybe she vacuum-cleans Melissa when she does the carpets,' grinned Dan.

Kitty giggled.

'That's enough,' said Dad.

There was a delicious smell of food when Aunty Susan opened the door. They all said Happy Christmas and hugged each other, although Daniel and Kitty ducked out of hugging their cousin.

'Why don't all the children play upstairs till dinner's ready?' said Uncle Joe.

But Dan asked if he could practise on his new skateboard on the garden path, and so Kitty was left with Melissa.

'Don't you like to wear your best dress on Christmas Day,' asked Melissa, 'instead of old jeans?'

'They aren't *old*, they're my new cords,' said Kitty indignantly. 'And this is a new jumper.'

'It wasn't a good start.

'Oh, well, I suppose you'd like to see all my presents,' said Melissa, throwing open her bedroom door.

Kitty gasped.

There was a toy cooker with plastic pots and pans, and a multi-way pram for Melissa's dolls, and a little pink wardrobe crammed with dolls' clothes on hangers, and a hairstyling set with pink plastic rollers, brushes and combs, and a funny dummy-head to work on.

'Who gave you all those?' asked Kitty.

'Mummy and Daddy. And I've got lots of

ordinary things like paints and books from
aunties and uncles.'

'Gosh,' said Kitty.

'What did you get?' asked Melissa.

Kitty told her.

'Is that *all*?' asked her cousin.

Suddenly Kitty felt like a balloon that has

gone pop. The turkey tasted delicious, and the crackers were fun, and Aunty Susan and Uncle Joe gave her a big notice-board in the shape of an elephant for her bedroom.

'So you can pin up your lists,' said Aunty Susan, picking up the paper right away and folding it neatly.

'Then you won't forget things,' smiled Uncle Joe.

Everybody laughed. Except Kitty.

At last it was time to go home. Kitty was glad to get back to their own comfortable, messy house. But Mum and Dad could tell that something was bothering her.

She sat by the Christmas tree, looking up at the coloured lights. And one thought was going through her mind – something so bad she wouldn't have told it to anyone. '*It's not fair she's got more presents than me.*' That was what Kitty thought.

Just then Dan came up. 'What did you think of Melissa's stuff then?' he asked.

'She had lots of nice presents,' said Kitty, in a small voice.

Daniel threw back his head and laughed. 'What? All those nimsy-mimsy things in pink plastic for dolly-wollies? Not your sort of thing, Kit. You've got more taste.'

And Kitty realised he was right. There wasn't a *single* thing in Melissa's room that she would have wanted. Not one.

She stared up at the tree again. It had a warm, Christmassy smell. Already, showers of little pine needles fell down when you touched it.

Aunty Susan had an artificial tree because she said real ones made too much mess. And they didn't have paper chains in each room, or a Christmas Candle in the window,

dropping wax all over the place, but giving a
warm welcoming glow.

Kitty grinned slowly.

'Our tree is *much* better than Melissa's
tree,' she said.

And *Melissa* might have said, 'Not fair!'

It's not fair!

I Have to do all the Work

'It's your turn.'

'No, it isn't. I did it yesterday.'

'But you said you'd make up for that time last week when you went out.'

'Nonsense.'

It wasn't Kitty and Daniel who were squabbling. It was Mum and Dad. And Kitty and Daniel couldn't bear it.

They were arguing over who did the washing-up. Usually they took turns, but lately things had got mixed up – and now they were very cross with each other.

'Tired! Huh! It's just not fair that I have to do all the work,' said Mum.

'What do you think I do all day?' said Dad.

And so they went on.

And on.

Kitty and Daniel were listening in the hall. 'I wish they'd shut up,' said Dan.

'So do I,' said Kitty. 'Why do parents have to argue?'

Daniel shrugged. 'Dunno . . . I suppose it's because they're just the same as us, underneath.'

Then Mum swept past them, slamming the kitchen door behind her. 'I'm going out to my class, kids,' she said. 'Bye.'

A few minutes later Dad stomped from the kitchen. 'You can start getting yourself to bed now, Kitty, and it's time you did your homework, Dan,' he said grumpily. 'I'm going out into the garage to mend the car radio.'

'All right, Dad,' they said together.

Five minutes later Kitty crept out of her bedroom. She knew what she had to do.

First she lifted up the laundry basket and half-carried, half-dragged it downstairs. One or two socks fell out along the way, but Kitty didn't notice.

In the kitchen she stuffed as many clothes as she could into the washing machine, and grabbed the powder. 'How much do you put in?' she wondered, then shrugged and poured a pile into the little compartment.

'One less job for Mum to do,' she said.

Then she took a chair and climbed up by the sink. A good, long squeeze of washing-up liquid . . . and a mountain of bubbles filled the sink. With a clatter Kitty swept all the dirty dishes into it.

Water and soap bubbles splashed on to the floor, but Kitty didn't mind. Her clothes were soaked, but it didn't matter. She piled all the washing-up anyhow on the draining-board, breaking just one cup. Only one. Then it was done. 'One less job for Dad to do,' she said.

What next? She looked around. The washing machine was making odd noises, and more bubbles were creeping from under its door. Never mind.

She decided to set the table ready for

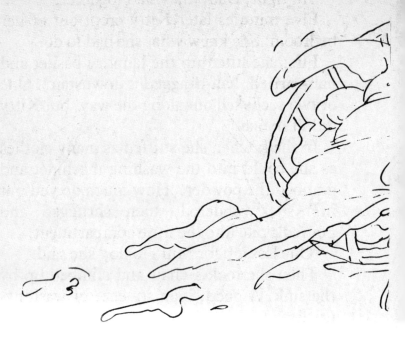

breakfast. But since all the usual dishes were on the draining-board in a *very* unsafe pile, she went to the sideboard and got out the best china and cutlery.

That was another job done. Now what? Mum was always saying the fridge needed a clear-out. So Kitty decided to do that – to be really helpful.

First you had to take everything out – but there was nowhere to put it really, except the table. And that was already laid for breakfast. Oh, never mind . . .

So Kitty put the milk bottles, orange

juice, butter, eggs, and everything else on the table amongst the best china. And only one egg got broken. Just one.

She wiped down the shelves, and then left the fridge and freezer doors open wide. She had seen Mum do that. That was another job they wouldn't have to do.

After that Kitty went into the sitting room and plumped up all the cushions, pummelling them furiously so that clouds of dust rose into the air.

She ran the carpet-sweeper over the hall carpet, but forgot to put it away.

She grabbed the feather duster and attacked
all the pictures, knocking most of them
sideways as she did so.

And when Mum came through the front
door, not long afterwards, Kitty was sitting
on the floor surrounded by a pile of shoes,
waving a brush, with polish all over her face
and hands – and a lot of it on the floor too.

Dad must have heard Mum, because just
then he came in through the back door.
'I just wanted to say I'm sor . . .'
he began, then stopped. He looked around
the kitchen in horror.

'What on earth has been going on?'
he said.

Kitty beamed. 'Well,' she said, 'I hate it when you argue. And since you both think it's not fair that you have to do so much work, I thought I'd help you. *I've* done all the work!'

Dad went across and put his arms around Mum, who looked as though she might faint. They stared at each other for a long time. And then they began to laugh. And laugh.

'Are you pleased?' asked Kitty.

'Y-y-yes, darling,' spluttered Mum.

'And so you promise you'll never argue again?' said Kitty wagging her finger at them.

'If you'll never do the work again. Fair enough!' said Dad.